THE BLACK AMERICAN JOURNEY

KETANJI BROWN JACKSON

SUPREME COURT JUSTICE

"So as I take on this new role, I strongly believe that this is a moment in which all Americans can take great pride."

— Ketanji Brown Jackson

BY EMILY DOLBEAR

Published by The Child's World®
800-599-READ • www.childsworld.com

Photography Credits

Cover and page 4: AP Photo/Jacquelyn Martin
Interior: Official White House Photo by Adam Schultz, 5, 6, 18, 25, 29 (right), 31; Allison Bailey/ZUMAPRESS/Newscom, 7; Courtesy of the Brown Family, 8; US National Archives and Records Administration, 9; Charles Pugh/*Atlanta Journal-Constitution* via AP, 10; AP Photo/Alex Brandon, 11; Debbie Herman/ *The Palm Echo* (1988)/Miami Palmetto Senior High School, 12, 28 (left); *The Palm Echo* (1988)/Miami Palmetto Senior High School, 13; Roman Babakin/ Shutterstock.com, 14; AP Photo/J. Scott Applewhite, 15, 17, 27, 28 (right); Steven Frame/Shutterstock.com, 16; stock_photo_world/Shutterstock.com, 19; Tom Williams/CQ Roll Call via AP Images/POOL, 20; Bill O'Leary/*The Washington Post* via Getty Images, 21; AP Photo/Pablo Martinez Monsivais, 22; US District Court for the District of Columbia, 23, 29 (left); AP Photo/Evan Vucci, 24; Supreme Court via AP, 26

ISBN Information
9781503880603 (Reinforced Library Binding)
9781503881914 (Portable Document Format)
9781503883222 (Online Multi-user eBook)
9781503884533 (Electronic Publication)

LCCN 2022949943

Printed in the United States of America

Cover and page 4 caption: Judge Ketanji Brown Jackson poses for a photograph in early 2022 while serving on the US Court of Appeals for the District of Columbia (DC) Circuit.

CONTENTS

Chapter One

A HISTORIC MOMENT

"On this vote, the yeas are 53, the nays are 47, and this **nomination** is confirmed," announced the vice president. Loud applause broke out on the Senate floor of the US Capitol. For almost a minute, many senators recognized the historic moment with clapping and cheers.

President Joe Biden and Ketanji Brown Jackson watch from the White House as the Senate votes on Jackson's confirmation to the Supreme Court.

Ketanji Brown Jackson and Kamala Harris share a moment on their way to a White House event. Harris is the first woman, first Black person, and first person of Asian descent elected vice president. Jackson is the first Black woman appointed to the Supreme Court.

A chief justice and eight **associate** justices sit on the **Supreme Court**. When a justice retires or dies, the president selects a new one. That person is called the nominee. The Senate needs to confirm, or approve, a nominee. More than half of the 100 members must say *yea* (pronounced "yay"). In the case of a 50-50 tie, the vice president has the deciding vote.

"All right!" cried the president in the White House some two miles away. He stood alongside the future 51-year-old Supreme Court **justice**, who smiled, hands clasped. They were watching the Senate vote on a large television screen in the Roosevelt Room. The two embraced; history had been made.

April 7, 2022, was indeed historic. A Black woman of Indian descent, Kamala Harris, had presided over the vote. And a Black woman had been elevated to the nation's highest court. Her name was Ketanji Brown Jackson.

Young people celebrate Ketanji Brown Jackson's historic confirmation to the Supreme Court at a rally in Washington, DC.

Chapter Two

KETANJI ONYIKA

Ketanji Onyika Brown was born in Washington, DC, on September 14, 1970. Johnny and Ellery Brown, her parents, gave her the African name *Ketanji Onyika*. It means "lovely one." The choice reflected pride in their roots and hope for what was to come. Their daughter Ketanji (pronounced "ke-TAHN-jee") would have rights they had not had.

Johnny and Ellery Brown had grown up in Miami, Florida, under **segregation**. They experienced it in libraries and parks, on buses, at restaurants, and also in their schools. At that time, Black students attended separate schools in many US states, mostly in the South.

Ketanji, with her mother, Ellery Brown, in the early 1970s, learned how to read when she was three years old.

Ketanji's parents attended segregated schools. Classrooms, like this one in Virginia in 1948, were overcrowded and underfunded.

In 1954, the Supreme Court decided that educating students by race was illegal. It had to stop. This decision, known as *Brown v. Board of Education,* was a huge step forward. It fueled the **civil rights movement**. Many, including the Browns, had hope for the future.

Education was a priority for the Browns. The couple were the first members of their families to attend college. They graduated from historically black colleges or universities (HBCUs). These school were set up before the Civil Rights Act of 1964 finally outlawed **discrimination** based on race. Both worked as public school teachers.

"Perhaps my earliest life lesson," Ketanji Brown Jackson said, "is the pride in my [roots] that my relatively unique name conveys." College friends remember her spelling out "Ketanji" when she met people to put them at ease.

Segregated public schools did not end right after the Supreme Court ruled against them in 1954. They persisted in southern states until the late 1960s.

When Ketanji was still young, her father decided on a new career—in the law. The Browns left Washington for Florida, and Johnny started at the University of Miami School of Law. Ketanji and her father often sat together at the kitchen table with their books (his for law; hers for coloring and later school). "We never deliberately set out . . . to instill in [our daughter] certain life lessons," Ketanji's father once explained. "We led by example."

Young people in Atlanta, Georgia, protest segregation at a cafeteria. Many civil rights activists in the early 1960s were college students who demanded an end to segregation.

Ketanji's parents, here in 2022, always encouraged their daughter's eagerness to learn.

And Ketanji's parents offered good examples. Her father was one of the first African Americans to graduate from his law school. He went on to serve as the attorney for the city school board. Ketanji's mother taught science in middle school. She was later **appointed** principal at a public high school for the arts. The Browns had high expectations for their family and valued work that helped others.

Chapter Three

GROWING UP

Ketanji thrived in school. She liked to write poems and play the piano, and she often carried a book with her. She enjoyed family time with aunts, uncles, cousins, and grandparents. Her brother, Ketajh, was born when she was nine. In Jackson's own words, her childhood was "terrific but normal."

The Browns lived in a largely Jewish community in South Miami with strong public schools. When it was time for high school, Ketanji was ready. She took challenging classes, was elected class president, and joined the speech and **debate** team.

In high school, Ketanji was elected class president three years in a row.

Ketanji, with a classmate in a 1988 yearbook photo, was a standout member of her high school speech and debate team.

Ketanji competed in speech and debate tournaments around the state and country. She delivered speeches and also performed dramatic and humorous pieces. As time went on, Ketanji grew more confident in writing and public speaking. It was, she says today, the "one activity that best prepared me for future success in law and in life." And it was with the team that she first visited Harvard University in Cambridge, Massachusetts.

When others underestimated her, Ketanji forged on. "As a dark-skinned Black girl who was often the only person of color in my class, club, or social environment," she explained later, "it was essential that I develop a sense of my own self-worth." Perhaps that's why, after her school counselor suggested Harvard was setting her sights too high, Ketanji applied anyway—and was accepted.

At high school speech and debate competitions, Ketanji Brown was nationally ranked. "The truth is—we are all timekeepers in our daily lives," she said in her speech. "And not only do we keep time—we buy it, spend it, borrow it, save it, kill it, conserve it, use it, and lose it within the course of every day."

When a classmate hung a flag considered a symbol of **racism** from his dorm window, Ketanji Brown protested with Harvard's Black Students Association. At the same time, she urged fellow members to stay focused on their studies.

She began at Harvard in the fall of 1988. It wasn't easy. At her confirmation hearing in 2022, Jackson was asked about believing in yourself when others may not. She responded with emotion: "I was walking through Harvard Yard my freshman year. . . . I was really homesick. I was really questioning: Do I belong here? Can I make it in this environment? And I was walking through the yard in the evening and a Black woman I did not know was passing me on the sidewalk and she looked at me, and I guess she knew how I was feeling, and she leaned over as we crossed and said 'Persevere.'"

Harvard University was founded in 1636. It is the oldest institution of higher education in the United States.

Ketanji and Patrick Jackson met while studying at Harvard.

Ketanji Brown did persevere, graduating from the school with honors in 1992. She had studied long hours, been active in the Black Students Association, participated in theater, and made lifelong friends. She even had a boyfriend, Patrick Jackson. His family had attended Harvard for six generations.

After a year off, reporting for *Time* magazine in New York City, Ketanji Brown returned to Harvard for a law degree. She continued to persevere, in her classes and as an editor of the *Harvard Law Review.*

Chapter Four

"HARD WORK, BIG BREAKS, AND TOUGH SKIN"

The year 1996 was important for Ketanji Brown. She graduated with honors from Harvard Law School. She married Patrick Jackson, who was then in training to be a surgeon. And she earned a **federal** clerkship, a yearlong position offered to the nation's top graduates.

The federal court system has three main levels: district courts, circuit courts, and the Supreme Court. There are 94 district, or trial, courts across the United States. If a **case** is lost in a district court, it can be **appealed**. That takes place in one of 12 regional circuit courts, or courts of appeals. The highest court of appeals is the US Supreme Court.

The Supreme Court Building in Washington, DC, was completed in 1935.

Judge Patti Saris is a district judge for the District of Massachusetts. Judge Saris hired Jackson as a law clerk right after she finished law school.

Jackson's first federal clerkship was at a district court in Boston. She worked for Judge Patti Saris. "[Jackson] had a sharp intellect and a warm, infectious smile," Judge Saris later said. "It was a no-brainer to hire her as a law clerk." Jackson did what law clerks do and did it well. She reviewed briefs (a brief is a written description of the facts of a case) and researched legal cases. And she helped write **opinions**.

Her next federal clerkship was at a circuit court in nearby Providence, Rhode Island. It was with Judge Bruce Selya of the US Court of Appeals for the First Circuit. In his words, as a law clerk, Jackson was "hardworking, dependable, intelligent, and most important, sensible."

In speeches to young people, Ketanji Brown Jackson often shares the following advice:

- Work hard at everything you're called upon to do.
- Show respect for other people.
- Be open to new ideas and experiences.
- Look for mentors and role models.

The third federal clerkship came in 1999. The Jacksons were back in Washington, DC. Patrick had a position there. Ketanji was working as an associate, or an entry-level professional. This job, better paid than one in government, would help pay off student loans.

Then came the chance she couldn't pass up—clerking at the Supreme Court for Justice Stephen Breyer. "Justice Breyer," she shared later, "plucked me from [nowhere] and gave me the opportunity of a lifetime." Jackson had now earned a clerkship at every level of the federal court system.

Stephen Breyer, nominated by President Bill Clinton in 1994, served as a Supreme Court justice for 28 years.

The nine justices of the Supreme Court are seated on the bench by seniority, and the public may sit to hear arguments.

Law clerks advise justices on the cases that come before the Supreme Court. Jackson quickly earned the respect of the other clerks for her intellect and lack of **bias**. She, in turn, saw the inner workings of the court and learned how justices reached agreement.

Clerking at the Supreme Court was an intense job. Jackson often worked 14 hours or more a day. "The stakes are so high," she has said. "But it was also just awe-inspiring every day." That year, the Supreme Court ruled on gay rights, prayer in public schools, and the rights of those in police custody.

After Jackson was nominated to the Supreme Court by President Biden, former law clerks who served the same term as Jackson sent a letter to the Senate Judiciary Committee: "We all support Judge Jackson's nomination to the Supreme Court," the group wrote, "because we know her to be eminently qualified for this role in intellect, character, and experience."

In her speeches, Jackson pays tribute to many women who came before her. She often speaks of Constance Baker Motley, the first Black woman to serve as a federal judge in 1966.

The following year, the Jacksons returned to Boston. Patrick had to finish his surgical training. Ketanji accepted a job in a large law firm.

Few women and even fewer women of color were working in the highest ranks of law firms. Once more, it wasn't easy. "I recall distinctly," Ketanji Brown Jackson said, "making the conscious decision to push forward [in the face of bias]." Working hard had always served her well, as had making the most of big opportunities. In speeches today, she refers to "hard work, big breaks, and tough skin."

Chapter Five

DREAM JOBS

Ketanji Brown Jackson gave birth to a daughter, Talia, in 2000. Like many new parents, she found family and career demanding. The rigid hours required to make partner at a law firm was not for her.

The young family moved to Washington, DC, for good in 2002. Patrick was now a surgeon. Ketanji worked at a private firm before turning again to public service. In 2003, she joined the staff of the US Sentencing Commission. This independent agency ensures that punishments for those found guilty of federal crimes are fair and just. The following year, the Jacksons welcomed a second daughter, Leila.

In 2005, Ketanji Brown Jackson took a job as a federal public defender. A public defender is a lawyer who represents **criminal defendants** unable to pay for one. "The rule of law requires that everyone's rights are respected," Jackson has said, "even people who can't afford a lawyer."

Ketanji Brown Jackson, here in 2019, has always valued public service, work that helps everyone.

Her cases were mostly appeals. For one, Jackson successfully argued that her client had been denied an unbiased **jury** during trial. "We have the fairest system of justice in the world, but it's not perfect," she once explained.

In 2007, Jackson returned to a law firm to handle appeals. The work was interesting. It was an excellent fit for her and her family.

Then, in 2009, Jackson received a call from the White House. President Barack Obama had selected her for vice chair of the US Sentencing Commission. This leadership post required Senate approval. Jackson began knitting. It calmed her nerves during the months-long process of earning her confirmation and seat.

President Barack Obama nominated Jackson to the US Sentencing Commission in 2009. He said she would be "an unwavering voice for justice and fairness on the Sentencing Commission."

Jackson became a federal judge—her dream job—in 2013.

At the urging of the US Sentencing Commission, Congress passed the Fair Sentencing Act in 2010. The law reduced unfair prison terms for certain drug crimes. The commission next took up allowing past defendants to seek reduced sentences. "I say justice demands this result," Vice Chair Jackson argued. The commission heard her words, and voted with one voice. The decision changed the lives of thousands in prison, most of whom were people of color.

Serving as a federal judge had always been Jackson's dream job. She got her shot at it in 2012. President Obama nominated her to the US District Court for the District of Columbia. Again, the position required Senate approval. This time, she knitted enough scarves for a small army.

It was Justice Breyer who swore Jackson into federal court in 2013. At the ceremony, her former boss remarked: "She sees things from different points of view, and she sees somebody else's point of view and understands it."

Ketanji Brown Jackson is the first Supreme Court justice to have served as a federal public defender.

Jackson's family members (Patrick, Leila, and Talia) listen during the Senate confirmation hearing on Capitol Hill. The hearing lasted four days.

Leila Jackson wrote a letter to the president, Barack Obama, when she was 11. In it, she recommended her mother for the Supreme Court. "She is determined, honest, and never breaks a promise to anyone, even if there are other things she'd rather do. She can demonstrate commitment, and is loyal and never brags."

Over the next eight years, Judge Ketanji Brown Jackson wrote more than 570 opinions. In 2018, she sided with the **unions** of federal workers. In 2019, she ruled that President Donald Trump could not keep his former White House lawyer from giving evidence. "No one is above the law," Jackson wrote. Then, in 2021, President Joe Biden nominated her to the US Court of Appeals for the DC Circuit.

Not long after, on February 25, 2022, President Biden nominated Judge Ketanji Brown Jackson to become the 116th justice of the Supreme Court. If approved, she would replace the retiring Stephen Breyer.

Chapter Six

HISTORIC DAYS

The day after Ketanji Brown Jackson was confirmed by the Senate, the White House held a small celebration. Staff, news reporters, and guests sat in folding chairs on the green grass of the South Lawn. Ketanji's parents, Johnny and Ellery Brown; her brother, Ketajh; and Patrick, Talia, and Leila were all there.

Jackson thanked her parents, who both grew up during segregation: "They, and so many others, did the heavy lifting that made this day possible. . . . I think of them as the true pathbreakers."

Jackson's brother, Ketajh Brown, served as a police detective in Baltimore, Maryland, and in the US Army in Iraq. He is now a lawyer.

Under a blue sky and sun, the justice-to-be gave thanks and acknowledged the past in her speech. "It has taken 232 years and 115 prior appointments for a Black woman to be selected to serve on the Supreme Court of the United States," she said, considering the weight of her own words. "But we've made it. We've made it, all of us."

Justice Stephen Breyer administers the judicial oath to Ketanji Brown Jackson as her husband holds two Bibles.

Members of the Supreme Court pose for their first group portrait after Justice Jackson's swearing in.

Justice Stephen Breyer officially retired on June 30, 2022. Just after noon on that historic day, Jackson was sworn in to replace him. Chief Justice John Roberts was in charge of the first **oath**, Justice Breyer the second. Jackson raised her right hand and placed the other on two Bibles, held by her husband. She swore to defend the **Constitution** "against all enemies" and "bear true faith and [loyalty] to the same." And then she pledged to "administer justice without respect to persons, and do equal right to the poor and to the rich."

Justice Ketanji Brown Jackson heard her first case as part of the Supreme Court on October 3.

Only five women before Ketanji Brown Jackson have served on the Supreme Court. The first two were Sandra Day O'Connor, from 1981 to 2006, and Ruth Bader Ginsburg, from 1993 until her death in 2020. Sonia Sotomayor, in 2009, became the third woman and first Hispanic to serve on the court. Elena Kagan took her seat in 2010 and Amy Coney Barrett in 2020. Only two Supreme Court justices have been men of color. Thurgood Marshall was on the bench from 1967 to 1991, when Clarence Thomas replaced him.

THINK ABOUT IT

Ketanji Brown Jackson is the first justice to have served as a public defender. Some people believe that this has given Jackson a better understanding of the justice system and the ways it impacts people's lives. Do you agree or disagree? Explain your reasoning.

Growing up in a mostly white community, Ketanji was often one of the few Black students in school. How was Ketanji's experience different from her classmates?

TIME LINE

1970 | 1980 | 1990

1970
Ketanji Onyika Brown is born on September 14 in Washington, DC.

1988
Ketanji Brown graduates from Miami Palmetto Senior High School, where she is class president and a star debater. She is accepted to Harvard University in Cambridge, Massachusetts.

1992
Ketanji Brown graduates from Harvard University. She takes a job as a reporter for *Time* magazine.

1993
Ketanji Brown attends Harvard Law School, serving as an editor of the *Harvard Law Review.*

1996
Ketanji Brown graduates from Harvard Law School. She marries Harvard classmate Patrick Jackson. She serves as a law clerk for Judge Patti Saris of the US District Court for the District of Massachusetts.

1997
Ketanji Brown Jackson clerks for Judge Bruce Selya of the US Court of Appeals for the First Circuit.

1999
Jackson serves as a law clerk at the Supreme Court for Justice Stephen Breyer.

For the first time in US history, there are four female justices sitting on the Supreme Court.
Is this significant, in your opinion? Do you think there will be a majority of women on the Supreme Court at some point? Why or why not?

All judges take an oath to be impartial.
In other words, they promise to treat everyone equally and not to show any biases. However, judges are regular people who have formed their own beliefs based on their experiences and identity. In your opinion, how does a judge's life experiences affect their ability to be unbiased?

2000

2003
Jackson joins the US Sentencing Commission, an independent agency that reviews federal sentencing guidelines.

2005
Jackson takes a job as a federal public defender in Washington, DC.

2010

2010
Jackson becomes vice chair of the US Sentencing Commission.

2013
Jackson is confirmed to the US District Court for the District of Columbia, after nomination by President Barack Obama in 2012.

2020

2021
Judge Jackson is confirmed to the US Court of Appeals for the DC Circuit, after nomination by President Joe Biden.

2022
President Biden nominates Judge Ketanji Brown Jackson to replace Stephen Breyer on the Supreme Court. The Senate confirms Jackson (53–47) on April 7. Jackson is sworn in as the 116th Supreme Court justice on June 30. Justice Jackson hears her first case on October 3. In November, Justice Jackson issues her first Supreme Court opinion.

appealed (uh-PEELD)
An appeal is a request for a higher court to hear a case. When a case is appealed, it is brought to a higher court to review the decision of a lower court.

appointed (uh-POYNT-ed)
When someone is appointed to a position, he or she is officially chosen and asked to accept.

associate (uh-SO-she-uht)
An associate is an entry-level member of a profession or organization. In the Supreme Court, all members are called associate justices, except for the chief justice, who presides over the court.

bias (BY-uhs)
Bias means an opinion that keeps a person from being fair. Jackson earned the respect of others for her intellect and lack of bias.

case (KASE)
A case is a matter for a court of law to decide. Jackson read and researched many cases during her federal clerkships.

civil rights movement (SIV-il RITES MOOV-munt)
The civil rights movement refers to the struggle for equal rights for Black Americans in the United States during the 1950s and 1960s.

Constitution (kon-stih-TOO-shun)
The US Constitution is the written document of the principles that govern the United States.

criminal defendants (KRIH-muh-nal dih-FEN-dunts)
Criminal defendants are people who are formally accused of a crime.

debate (deh-BAYT)
A debate is a discussion between people with different opinions on a subject. Ketanji joined her high school's speech and debate team.

discrimination (diss-krim-ih-NAY-shun)
Discrimination is unfair treatment of people based on differences of race, gender, religion, or culture. Discrimination based on race was outlawed after the Civil Rights Act of 1964 was passed.

federal (FED-er-uhl)
Federal means having to do with the nation's central government, rather than a state of city government. Jackson earned a federal clerkship after graduating from Harvard Law School.

jury (JEHR-ee)
A jury is a group of people in a court of law who listen to the facts of a case and decide on its outcome. A member of a jury must be unbiased to ensure that a case is handled fairly.

justice (JUSS-tiss)
A justice is a judge. Jackson became the 116th Supreme Court justice in 2022.

nomination (NAH-muh-nay-shun)
A nomination is the act of choosing a person for a position. President Biden nominated Judge Jackson to replace Stephen Breyer on the Supreme Court.

oath (OHTH)
An oath is a solemn promise. All judges take an oath of office before they become Supreme Court justices.

opinions (uh-PIN-yuhnz)
Opinions are written legal rulings. During her clerkship, Jackson researched cases and helped write opinions.

racism (RAY-sih-zum)
Racism is the belief that one race is superior to another. Ketanji protested against racism when she was a college student.

segregation (seg-ruh-GAY-shun)
Segregation is the practice of using laws to keep groups of people apart. Segregation was still legal when Jackson's parents, Ellery and Johnny, were growing up.

Supreme Court (suh-PREEM KORT)
The Supreme Court is the highest court in the United States. It is made up of a chief justice and eight associate justices.

unions (YOON-yuns)
Unions are organizations of workers formed to improve pay, benefits, and working conditions. As a judge, Jackson ruled on cases involving unions.

BOOKS

Moses, Shelia P., and Dede Putra (illustrator). *Who Is Ketanji Brown Jackson?* New York, NY: Penguin Workshop, 2022.

Rubinstein, Justine. *The Supreme Court*. Philadelphia, PA: Mason Crest, 2020.

Schwartz, Heather E. *Ketanji Brown Jackson: First Black Woman on the US Supreme Court*. Minneapolis, MN: Lerner, 2023.

Venable, Rose. *The Civil Rights Movement*. Mankato, MN: The Child's World, 2021.

Weatherford, Carole Boston, and Ashley Evans (illustrator). *All Rise: The Story of Ketanji Brown Jackson*. New York, NY: Crown Books for Young Readers, 2023.

Weston, Margeaux. *20th Century African American History for Kids: The Major Events That Shaped the Past and Present*. Emeryville, CA: Rockridge Press, 2021.

WEBSITES

Visit our website for links about Ketanji Brown Jackson:

childsworld.com/links

Note to Parents, Caregivers, Teachers, and Librarians: We routinely verify our Web links to make sure they are safe, active sites—so encourage your readers to check them out!

INDEX